Penguin Club

Written and Illustrated by Zoe Carter

Copyright Zoe Carter 2019

The Bible is a great big library. Sixty-six books in all. Some are big and some are small.

Books about the past, books about the future, letters, poems, stories that are true. And all of the books are from God to you.

Let's take a look at the book of Hebrews.

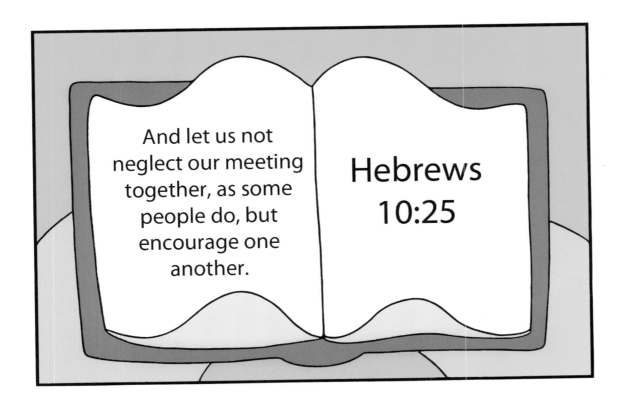

And let us not neglect our meeting together, as some people do, but encourage one another.

Hebrews 10:25

'I don't understand', said Little Mole.

'To help us think, why don't we have a dig?'

'And as we dig, let me tell you a story.'

It was time for Penguin Club!
Penny couldn't wait!

She put on her hat.

She slid out of her igloo

and she waddled along to the group.

But when she got there, Penny found that Penguin Club was not quite as fun as she remembered.

Someone squawked in her ear.

When someone caught a fish
it landed on her head.

Someone pushed her over on the ice rink.

Someone catapulted her out of her kayak.

Someone knocked over her ice cream.

She came last in the wheelbarrow race because her partner was not playing properly.

And when someone sat on her artwork,
this was the last straw.

Penny had enough. 'I am leaving Penguin Club!' she declared, as she threw her hat on the ground.

And with that, she waddled away from the group.

'What a silly club!' she said to herself.

She held out her flippers as it started to snow.

'I am like a snowflake, individual and unique.'

'I don't need those other penguins.
I'm better off alone.'

But as the day turned to night,
Penny started to feel cold and lonely.

She tripped on a stick and she fell.

She had no one to help her up.

And as the snow settled on her she lost hope.

The next morning Wendy Walrus built a snowman.
'Look Daddy!', she said.

'Hmm. There's something funny about this
snowman', said Daddy Walrus.

'I knew it!' he said, as he pulled up Penny.
'It's an upside-down penguin!'

'And she is frozen solid.'

Penny knew what she had to do. 'Please may you take me back to Penguin Club?' she asked.

'Of course!' said Daddy Walrus. He put Wendy on his back, he picked up Penny, and they bounced back to Penguin Club.

The penguins were so happy to see Penny.
They huddled around her to help her warm up.

And as they huddled, Penny's ice started to melt, and she began to defrost.

They gave Penny her hat back.

Penny explained to the penguins why she had left. They knew the club had become chaotic, but they had no idea how upset she had felt.

They decided to make a change. They voted for a sensible penguin to be their captain.

They gave him a special hat and a whistle.

So that when things started to go wrong...

he could put a stop to it.

and make sure that everyone was OK.

The penguins tried much harder
to look after one another

and to help each other.

And when they had done wrong, they tried to make it right.

Sometimes accidents would happen.

But Penny learned to forgive and move on.

They all worked to make Penguin Club a place
where people wanted to be,

so that they could stay together, and keep out the cold.

THE END

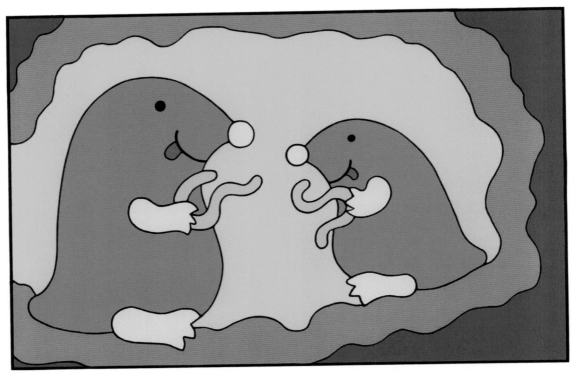

The story helped Little Mole understand why it's important to stick together. The moles had dug so deep, that they found some delicious worms.

Make allowance for each other's faults, and forgive anyone who offends you.

Colossians 3:13

Zoe Carter lives in Edinburgh, the capital of Scotland. She loves to make puppets, drink tea with her friends, and dress up in fancy dress costumes. Her favourite animal is an octopus.

www.zoecraftbook.com

Check out Zoe's Bible craft activity website www.zoecraftbook.com
More than 100 craft activities with full step by step photographic
instructions and templates. Fun, high quality and easy. Suitable for boys
and girls. Ideal for Sunday school, church, holiday clubs, homeschooling,
family time, VBS, camps, away days and many more.

Other titles by Zoe Carter

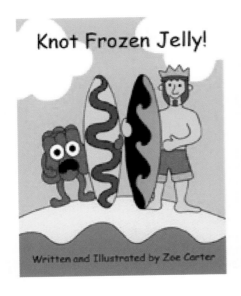

Knot Frozen Jelly!

Written and Illustrated by Zoe Carter

Sir Lived Alot

A story about Ecclesiastes by Zoe Carter

Silly Billy

A story based on the book of Proverbs
Written and illustrated by Zoe Carter

Matthew Mouse

A story based on Proverbs
by Zoe Carter

Rachel Rabbit
Zoe Carter

The Fish Tank

Written and Illustrated by Zoe Carter

And many more

Available now from Amazon

Printed in Great Britain
by Amazon